Solves a Crime

PAMELA
BUTCHART

illustrated by
GEMMA
CORRELL

nosy
crow

Wigglesbottom Primary:

The Toilet Ghost

The Shark in the Pool

The Magic Hamster

Illustrated by Becka Moor

Baby Aliens Got My Teacher!

The Spy Who Loved School Dinners

My Head Teacher is a Vampire Rat!

Attack of the Demon Dinner Ladies

To Wee Or Not to Wee!

Illustrated by Thomas Flintham

To Roz and Gavin.
Happy Wedding Day!

P. B.

First published in the UK in 2016 by Nosy Crow Ltd
The Crow's Nest, 10a Lant Street
London, SE1 1QR, UK

Nosy Crow and associated logos are trademarks and/or registered
trademarks of Nosy Crow Ltd

Text copyright © Pamela Butchart, 2016
Cover and illustrations copyright © Gemma Correll, 2016

The right of Pamela Butchart and Gemma Correll to be identified
as the author and illustrator respectively of this work has been asserted
by them in accordance with the Copyright, Designs
and Patents Act 1988.

Printed and bound in the UK by Clays Ltd, St. Ives Plc

Papers used by Nosy Crow are made from wood grown in
sustainable forests.

ISBN: 978 0 85763 676 8

www.nosycrow.com

Chapter 1

As soon as I saw the neighbour's new dog  I just KNEW that she was going to be TROUBLE.

I mean, she's a POODLE and EVERYONE knows that poodles can't be trusted. They're too bouncy and pood-ly.

I'm a pug and pugs are NOTHING like poodles!

Pugs are BRAVE

and CREATIVE

and probably # GENIUSES

and poodles are NONE
of those things!

Clem lives in the same house as I do. But she's not a poodle OR a pug. She's a cat! Clem likes to pretend she doesn't like me (but I know she does!).

Clem is

SUPER SMART

(but sometimes she is

SUPER MOANY).

Clem said I was
being SILLY
and that poodles
were totally
HARMLESS and
had candy floss
for brains.

So I explained that that's EXACTLY what poodles WANT everyone to think and that they are actually EVIL GENIUSES.

But Clem just ROLLED HER EYES (like she ALWAYS does) and said that she didn't think a dog called GLITTERPUFF could be evil OR a genius.

But then LOADS of stuff began mysteriously DISAPPEARING. Like Maddy's (that's our owner) favourite jumper with the orange pumpkins on it, and LOADS of Tiny the chihuahua's favourite things.

But it was when I heard that Big Sal the guinea pig had been GUINEA PIG-NAPPED that I knew it was time for me to become a PUG-TECTIVE!

Chapter 2

I told Clem that she should be my assistant and that she could answer the phone and take notes and bring me snacks.

Once Clem EVENTUALLY stopped rolling around on the floor laughing she said, "I will be the DIRECTOR of the detective agency."

I didn't really know what a DIRECTOR was, but Clem said that it meant she would be in charge and WATCH OVER the investigation and

ALL FUTURE INVESTIGATIONS.

So I said OK because I needed someone to watch me VERY CLOSELY to make sure I didn't lose my hat because EVERY good detective needs a HAT. And when crimes DON'T get solved it probably isn't because the detective can't find any clues; it's probably because he forgot to wear his hat!

Clem said that the HAT THING was STUPID. So I ran around and barked and threw myself against the sofa for AGES because I was having a

PUG-TANTRUM.

"Are you quite finished?" said Clem, holding something up.

"What's that?" I said.

"While you were being

RIDICULOUS

I made a list of VICTIMS. We're going to interview everyone who's had something stolen and start investigating."

"You are right, Clem," I said. "And we must also look for CLUES!"

So we waited until Maddy went off to school and then I raced into the bathroom and pushed the window open. Then Clem and I were off to solve our first ever CASE!

Chapter 3

Our first interview was with Tiny the Chihuahua. As we waited for her to open the door there seemed to be a weird wailing coming from inside the house.

"Oh!" said Tiny, poking her head out of the door. "I wasn't expecting company." She looked a bit weird.

"Were you just wailing?" I asked her.

"No," she said.

"I thought I heard a wailing coming from inside but it's stopped now."

"Oh, actually, YES! That was me!" said Tiny. "I … er … forgot."

Then as soon as I showed Tiny my homemade detective's badge she BURST out crying.

"Thank GOODNESS you're here!" she shrieked. "I've been horribly ROBBED!" And then she dropped to the ground and kicked her little chihuahua legs in the air.

"That nasty thief has stolen my orange scarf AND my best tartan jacket and loads of my hairdressing stuff! Those are ALL of my favourite things, Pugly! ALL OF MY FAVOURITES! WHAAAAAAAAAAAAAAAAA!"

Clem narrowed her eyes as Tiny flopped

around from side-to-side on the carpet and then she wrote something down on her INVESTIGATION PAD.

"Can you tell us if you saw anything SUSPICIOUS the night your belongings were stolen?" said Clem.

"I DEFINITELY DID!" said Tiny. And then she started whimpering and shaking LOADS.

So I put a blanket over her shoulders because that's the sort of stuff detectives do when they are trying to help the victims.

Tiny wrapped herself up tight in the blanket so that only her face was poking out. She looked TERRIFIED!

"I saw a footprint..." she whispered. "A seriously

BIG

FOOTPRINT!"

Clem's tail began flicking from side to side.

"Can you show us this footprint, please?" she asked.

Tiny's eyes started to go WEIRD and I just KNEW that she was about to faint so I lay her down on the sofa and brought her water bowl over.

"Straw, please," whimpered Tiny as her little chihuahua arm flopped over the side of the sofa.

We waited until she was HYDRATED because dogs can't really speak when they need water because of all the panting.

"Aaaah! That's better," said Tiny. "I'm afraid the footprint is gone. The rain took it away."

So I got some pens out of my bag and asked Tiny if she could DRAW the footprint for us. Tiny spent

AGES

looking through my pens until she eventually picked an orange one. But the drawing wasn't very good because her little paws were too shaky.

"And I saw a SHADOW, too!"
she said. "I think it was
a WOLF!" That's when
I started shaking a bit, too,
because I REALLY didn't want
the thief to be a WOLF because
WOLVES are TOO SCARY!

"What about a POODLE, Tiny?" I asked, hopefully. "Do you think it could have been a really big and evil poodle?"

Clem looked at me and rolled her eyes.

"Maybe," said Tiny. "But it would have had to be a really, REALLY evil one!"

"I see," said Clem. "And is there anything ELSE you'd like to tell us, Tiny?"

That's when I noticed that Clem's tail was flicking LOADS so I knew that she was annoyed at something but I wasn't sure what.

"No, that's everything," said Tiny, and she suddenly jumped to her feet and began to fold her blanket up nicely.

Clem snapped her notebook shut. Then she paused. "One more thing. We got word that Big Sal the guinea pig is missing. Do you know anything about that?" She narrowed her eyes and stared at Tiny.

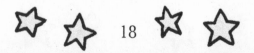

"Nope," said Tiny. "Bye bye."

And she pushed us out of the door before I even had a chance to say goodbye.

"I don't trust that chihuahua!" Clem hissed at me once we were outside. "She's too DRAMATIC. She's going on the

SUSPECT LIST."

I looked up and saw Tiny at her window, staring at us. I raised my paw to wave but just then she shut the curtains.

"Clem," I said patiently. "You should just leave all the detective stuff to me from now on as you are obviously a TERRIBLE detective who can't tell the difference between a VICTIM and a CRIMINAL. I mean, Tiny cried REAL TEARS and everything!"

Clem looked like she was going to KILL ME. So I shouted, "Let's get to the next CRIME SCENE!" And ran off before she could get me.

Chapter 4

When we got to Big Sal's house it was OBVIOUS something bad had happened there.

Sal's hutch door was WIDE OPEN and his food bowl had spilled EVERYWHERE.

"DON'T MOVE A CAT MUSCLE!"

I said. "I need to dust for PAW PRINTS!"

I was so EXCITED to get the chance to use my DETECTIVE KIT.

I opened the briefcase I'd taken from Maddy's dad's wardrobe and took out some flour and ALL of Maddy's mum's make-up brushes.

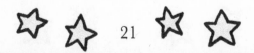

I opened the flour and then spun round and round until it was

EVERYWHERE.

"URRRGGGGGH! PUGLY! What are you DOING?!" said Clem. "You've COVERED me in FLOUR!"

But I didn't have time to answer because
I was too busy dusting for PAW PRINTS!
And THAT'S when I found my first
CLUE. It was a LONG WHITE HAIR.

"GET ME
A SANDWICH BAG!"

I yelled.

Once the hair was secured inside the sandwich bag, Clem wrote

CLUE NUMBER ONE

on the bag and then we both INSPECTED the hair closely.

"There's NO WAY this belongs to Big Sal," said Clem. "Big Sal is completely ORANGE."

"It's a REALLY long hair, Clem," I said, nervously. "You don't think Tiny might have been right about the WOLF, do you?"

Just then Chester popped his head over the fence and gave us both a HUGE fright. "Hey, dudes. Do you like my new hair?"

Chester is a DOG MODEL and he is TOTALLY OBSESSED with his hair! Usually it's brown but today he had loads of WHITE HIGHLIGHTS!

"Pretty groovy, huh? I'm shooting a TV ad for 'Yeah Veg!' dog food tomorrow. What are you guys doing here?"

Clem opened her notepad and wrote

SUSPECT
NUMBER TWO

across the top and gave me a LOOK. I knew she wanted me to INTERVIEW CHESTER.

"Hi, Chester," I said. "My hat should tell you that I am a

FAMOUS DETECTIVE

and we are investigating all the STEALING that's been going on."

"Good for you, man," said Chester. "Someone stole my funky new modelling outfit. It's messed up."

"Your hair is very long these days," said Clem, flicking her tail about.

And that's when Chester jumped RIGHT over the fence and talked for AGES because Chester

♡ LOVES ♡

talking about his hair.

"I KNOW, man! I've been growing it, like, FOR EVER!"

"Oh, I love it when you swish your hair around like that," purred Clem. "I'd love to have a photo of you so I can remember how swishy it is."

Chester almost BURST with excitement.

"SURE! I'll go grab my camera," he said and he leapt back over the fence.

"QUICK!" hissed Clem. "Help me pick up all this hair and BAG IT before he gets back!"

Then I realised why Clem was being so nice to Chester! She wanted some of his HAIR to see if it matched the one we found at Big Sal's hutch. One day she would be as great a detective as

ME!

Chapter 5

As soon as we got back to the house, I took out the hair we found in Big Sal's hutch and lined it up next to one of Chester's. But it WASN'T a match.

Chester's hair was MUCH longer than the one from the hutch, which didn't really look white any more. It looked a bit SILVERY and GREY.

Clem stared at me and said, "It looks like Tiny might have been right after all. Maybe it WAS a wolf!"

I totally FREAKED OUT and hid inside the washing basket and waited for Clem to come and make me feel better. That is what I like to do when I'm scared.

But Clem didn't come.

So I shouted, "CLEM! CLEM! CLEM! CLEM! CLEM! CLEM! CLEM!"

Clem began pulling me out of the washing basket. She was a bit angry because I'd woken her from a nap. "Pugly. Detectives don't HIDE when things get scary. They have to be BRAVE."

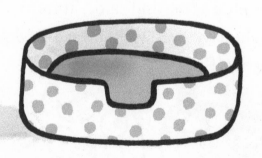

And that's when I KNEW that Clem was right. I leaped out of the washing basket and stood up straight with my hands on my hips. "I am a detective and I am BRAVE!"

Clem burst out laughing and pointed to my head. I looked in the mirror and saw I had frilly pants stuck to my hat.

Then the doorbell rang and I almost JUMPED out of my fur!

"How BRAVE," said Clem, as she went to peek through the letterbox.

"Who is it?" she asked. And then she HISSED. That's when I KNEW it must be ANOTHER CAT!

"The name's Carlos," I heard the visitor say. "Word on the street is you've got an investigation on the go. I have some information I believe might be of interest to you."

Clem's eyes went wide. "Cat flap's round the back," she said.

"Nice place you've got here," said Carlos as he wandered around our kitchen. "Shame about the pug."

"HEY!" I snapped.

Carlos jumped up on the kitchen counter and began sniffing around near MY biscuit tin.

"You said you had some information for us?" said Clem.

"Maybe I do. Maybe I don't," said Carlos. "What's it worth?"

That's when I noticed that Carlos didn't have a collar on.

"Hey, Carlos. I think you've lost your collar," I said. "Maybe you should GO AWAY and find it." I didn't like this cat

ONE BIT

and I DEFINITELY didn't want his help in

MY investigation.

Carlos jumped down from the counter and came RIGHT up to my face.

"Don't HAVE a collar," he said, grinning. "Don't NEED one."

And that's when I realised that Carlos was a STRAY CAT and stray cats can be DANGEROUS and some of them are in

CAT GANGS

and they get up to NO GOOD and I know that for a fact because Maddy and I watched a programme all about it.

CATZ
RULE

CATZ

I looked at Clem and GULPED because even CLEM is a bit scared of stray cats.

"Live by my own rules, see," said Carlos. "Don't need no stinking collar. OR home. OR silly HUMAN telling me what to do. I'm my OWN boss."

"What do you want?" said Clem.

Carlos turned and smiled slyly at her. "Those DOGGY biscuits look nice. I think I'd like them ALL."

That's when I started to feel dizzy. He wanted MY doggy biscuits.

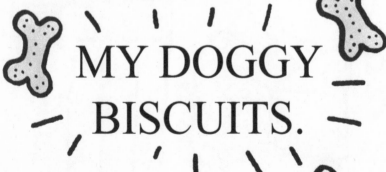

MY DOGGY BISCUITS.

ALL of them!
I slumped to the ground.

"Hey, what's wrong with the pooch?" said Carlos.

"Don't worry about him," said Clem. "I'm sure he'll feel better once you tell us what you know."

"Not so fast. FIRST you give me the doggy biscuits. THEN I give you the info."

"Clem, NO!" I barked, still lying on the floor. "He's going to eat ALL of my biscuits and then tell us NOTHING!"

Carlos grinned.

Clem jumped on to the counter and knocked my doggy treats to the floor and I had to watch between my paws as Carlos ate EVERY SINGLE LAST ONE. I almost cried. They smelled DELICIOUS.

Carlos licked his lips and yawned. "OK, SEE YA!" he said, making for the door.

"Not so fast," said Clem, stepping in front of the cat flap. "That pug might look like a chubby nitwit—"

"HEY!" I shouted.

Clem gave me a look. "But he's got a nasty temper. And you've made him angry and HUNGRY."

That's when Clem did her WIDEST EYES EVER at me and I realised what she wanted me to do.

"YEAH! I'm HUNGRY! And MAD!" I said, and then I did my SCARIEST PUG FACE at Carlos. But he just laughed.

"You know, you'd look a LOT scarier if you didn't have that silly hat on."

And then suddenly I really WAS angry! I completely

LOST IT.

I started barking and growling and running into EVERYTHING because Carlos had made fun of my AWESOME DETECTIVE'S HAT!

Carlos looked TERRIFIED.
He started hissing and wailing
and trying to get out of the cat
flap but Clem wouldn't budge.

"Start talking!" she yelled.

"It's that weird poodle,
Glitterpuff," said Carlos. "She's
been sneaking out of her house
every night this week. She's
definitely up to something.
Now let me out!"

"Thank you," said Clem, and
then she stood aside and Carlos
scarpered out the cat flap.

Chapter 6

"I KNEW IT!" I yelled at Clem. "I TOLD YOU that poodle was BAD NEWS!"

But Clem STILL didn't look convinced. Even after everything that Carlos had told us!

Then Clem said, "Poodles have CURLY hair, Pugly."

And I GASPED because the long, grey hair we found was completely STRAIGHT. But that's when I got a

BRAIN PING,

which is what happens when I get a

PUGTASTIC IDEA.

It's sort of like a microwave pinging,
but in my head. And I yelled, "HAIR
STRAIGHTENERS, Clem! Glitterpuff
is DEFINITELY the type of dog who has
HAIR STRAIGHTENERS! She could have
had STRAIGHT hair the night she stole
Big Sal!"

We knocked on Glitterpuff's kennel door for AGES before she eventually poked her head out a tiny bit.

"May we come in, please?" I said. And then I shoved my tinfoil detective's badge RIGHT in her face so she would know that this was

SERIOUS.

"No. I'm busy!" she snapped and then she slammed the kennel door and we heard the lock snap shut.

"Well, THAT was rude. And very SUSPICIOUS," I said.

I banged on the kennel door for AGES until that annoying poodle poked her head out again. "GO AWAY! I don't have time for this TODAY OF ALL DAYS!"

"Why not?" I asked, looking at the

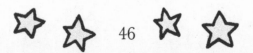

towel wrapped around Glitterpuff's head. "Are you COLOURING your hair? And I suppose you've got some HAIR STRAIGHTENERS in there too, haven't you?"

"Colouring my hair?!" cried Glitterpuff. "Of COURSE I'm not! I'm DEFINITELY not going anywhere special later! I'm staying in ALL NIGHT to watch TV. Goodbye!"

And then she slammed the door shut again.

"She's lying," said Clem. "I saw a bit of PINK HAIR sticking out of her towel! You were RIGHT about that poodle."

"She's covering her tracks, Clem. If she has PINK CURLY hair, we can't match it to the hair we found in Big Sal's hutch at the CRIME SCENE.

SHE
IS
AN
EVIL GENIUS!"

But I wasn't going to let a poodle get the better of me. ESPECIALLY a poodle who was a thief AND a guinea pig-napper!

And that's when I came up with the most BRILLIANT and PROFESSIONAL detective plan

EVER!

Chapter 7

It was my idea to do the STEAK-OUT. I was

MEGA EXCITED

because a STEAK-OUT is when you sit in a car outside a SUSPECT'S house until the suspect MAKES THEIR MOVE and then you follow them and find out what they're up to.

"But what happens if Glitterpuff doesn't come out for AGES?" said Clem.

So I explained that that's why it's called a STEAK-OUT because you take lots of food

(like steak!) OUTSIDE with you so you
don't get hungry if you're there all night.

And I showed her my bag with the
HUGE steak from the fridge in it and some
donuts too.

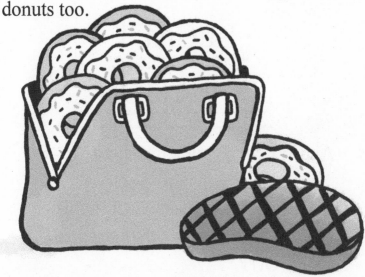

That's when Clem said that a STAKE-
OUT wasn't about STEAK and also that I
had got my spellings a bit mixed up. But
she agreed that it was a

GREAT DETECTIVE IDEA!

We knew that Glitterpuff had been lying about staying in to watch TV that night. She was obviously going to sneak off to steal more stuff and hide it in a

SECRET

LOCATION.

And WE were going to follow her.

Clem was NOT pleased when I told her that I'd asked Chester to help us do the STAKE-OUT.

But I explained that we might need someone to KEEP WATCH if we decided to search the kennel once Glitterpuff left. Then as soon as Chester arrived we sneaked up and down the street until we found a car with the window left open a bit. It was RIGHT outside Glitterpuff's house so it was the PERFECT stake-out spot!

Clem slipped through the little gap and then unlocked the doors and we jumped in when no one was looking.

"This is awesome, man!" said Chester as he munched on a donut. "We're like the cops.

 I LOVE IT!

So who's the dude we're spying on?"

"It's Glitterpuff," I said. "We think she might have something to do with Big Sal's disappearance."

Chester's face went a funny shape and he dropped the donut on the floor. Then he began acting TOTALLY WEIRD and saying that he couldn't help us any more.

He tried to get out of the car but Clem had already hit the locks.

"Look, dudes … you GOTTA let me out!"

Clem's eyes went

"What's wrong, Chester? Why don't you want to help us?" I asked.

Chester began nervously playing with his hair.

"You KNOW something!" said Clem. She leapt into the backseat and went right up to Chester's face.

"You KNOW who the THIEF is, don't you? You're PROTECTING them. Or maybe it's YOU, Chester!"

"DUDES! I SWEAR on all the 'Yeah Veg' dog food in the world I've got

NO IDEA

who's taking the stuff. It

DEFINITELY

isn't ME!

I'd NEVER kidnap Big Sal! I'm sorta TERRIFIED of that little dude! He's scary, even though he's got ladies' hair."

Clem chuckled. "How can you be

SCARED

of a little orange guinea pig?"

"Hey, Big Sal is no joke! And he's got a LOT of friends, you know? I don't wanna get involved, man. You're on your own, Señoritas!"

And then before me or Clem could stop him Chester rolled down the window and leapt out.

"Hey, CHESTER! COME BACK! HEY!!" Clem shouted after him.

"SSSSSSSSSHHHHHHH, CLEM!" I hissed. "You'll blow our COVER! LOOK, there's Glitterpuff now!" And then I dragged Clem to the floor so Glitterpuff wouldn't see us.

"GET OFF ME!" hissed Clem. "YOUR

BREATH STINKS! And now I'm
COVERED in donuts!"

"Let's GO!" I whispered, ignoring the
insults. "It's time to follow the SUSPECT!"

Chapter 8

We watched as Glitterpuff tiptoed down the driveway.

She was wearing a long, dark coat with a hood that completely covered her head. But we knew it was her because we recognised her feet and her PAINTED TOENAILS.

We followed Glitterpuff for AGES. And we had to sometimes DIVE behind bins and trees because she kept stopping and looking behind her.

All of a sudden, Glitterpuff changed direction and darted straight into the dark park.

"Clem!" I hissed. "I can't go in there. It's COMPLETELY BLACK!"

Clem sighed. Then she grabbed my collar and pulled me into the park anyway.

It was HORRIBLE. I couldn't see a thing
and the ground was wet and something felt
yucky under my paws, like SLIME or CAT
POO.

I kept really close to Clem because
she can see much better in the dark than
me. But then she stopped suddenly and I
crashed into her and yelped with fright.

Then someone started laughing.

And I COMPLETELY FROZE.

"Well, well. Fancy seeing you two here,"
said a voice.

"CLEM!" I yelled. "There are GHOSTS
IN THIS PARK!"

   And THAT'S when I looked up and saw
two things shining in the nearest tree!
GHOST EYES! And then LOADS of
GHOST EYES appeared ALL AROUND
US!

   I heard Clem gulp. "Those aren't ghost
eyes, Pugly."

   And as soon as Clem said that, the
WAILING started and I realised that the
shining eyes were CAT EYES and that
it was CARLOS and his STRAY CAT
GANG!

   So we ran.

Chapter 9

As soon as we reached the far end of the park we collapsed on to the pavement under a street lamp to catch our breath.

That's when I realised that it was

The investigation. Catching Glitterpuff.
My entire career and life as a detective.

I'd lost my hat in the park.

"Just LEAVE IT!" said Clem. "You don't
need it."

I was explaining to Clem that I definitely
DID need it and about how all great
detectives NEED their hats when I saw
a pair of white legs disappear through a
church window.

"Glitterpuff!" I whispered.

We ran up the church path and Clem
jumped up on to the window ledge and
looked inside. She gave a little yelp of
surprise.

"What's going on?" I asked, frantically jumping up and down and trying to see in. But my pug legs were far too short.

"Erm. It's hard to describe…" said Clem.

"What do you mean? Can you see Glitterpuff?"

"Oh, I can see Glitterpuff all right. EVERYONE can!"

I was desperate to know what was going on! "What is she doing? And who is EVERYONE?!"

Just then there was a really loud HOWL.

"C-c-c-clem," I stuttered. "Pu-pu-pu-pleeeeease don't say there's a GREY WOLF in there!"

Just then the church doors flew open and Glitterpuff came running out. Her hair was bright PINK and she was wearing a WEDDING DRESS.

She was also howling and she had tears

streaming down her long nose.

"Where is my FIANCE?!" she wailed.

The church doors flew open again. And I almost weed myself because I thought it was a GREY WOLF.

But it wasn't.

It was hundreds of GUINEA PIGS!

Chapter 10

There were guinea pigs EVERYWHERE. And some of them were wearing TOP HATS which looked AWESOME (but also made me a bit sad because it reminded me of losing MY hat).

All the guinea pigs clustered around
Glitterpuff and patted her legs comfortingly
while she howled and said stuff like, "How
could this happen to ME?" and "He is the
long-haired love of my LIFE!" and "Is it
because I'm taller than him?"

I turned to Clem. Her mouth was literally
hanging

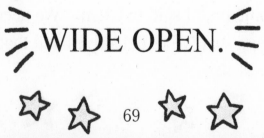

WIDE OPEN.

I wasn't surprised because it was obvious that Glitterpuff was talking about BIG SAL.

GLITTERPUFF AND
BIG SAL WERE
GETTING MARRIED!

"WHERE IS HE?"

howled Glitterpuff.

All the guinea pigs looked up at Glitterpuff. Some looked sad. Some looked furious. And one of them was stamping on his top hat.

"Come on," I said to Clem. "We need to tell them that we're detectives and that we

can help rescue Big Sal from the guinea pig-napper!"

"Pugly, wait! I don't think Big Sal has been guinea pig-napped. Maybe he ran away?"

"But why would Big Sal run away the night before his own WEDDING?!"

Clem jumped down from the window ledge and whispered in my ear.

"Because maybe he doesn't WANT to marry Glitterpuff after all. He's left her standing at the altar, Pugly."

I looked over at Glitterpuff. She threw her bouquet of flowers to the ground and then rolled all over them until they were smushed.

Maybe Clem was right. Glitterpuff seemed mad. And so did everyone else.

Just then, Chester came bounding over.

"Dudes! Sorry about running away, that was uncool. But Big Sal made me promise not to tell anyone about the wedding. It's so rad – the first poodle-guinea pig wedding EVER! But, like, they didn't want all the press turning up so it had to be totally hush-hush, you dig?"

"That's why you didn't want to help us spy on Glitterpuff," said Clem.

"Yeah, man," said Chester. "She's been going off at night to see her wedding planner. And she NO WAY had kidnapped Big Sal. When you said the little dude was gone, I TOTALLY just thought he was off partying with his buddies. Those guinea pigs LOVE their disco dancing!"

But then Chester wiped a tear from his eye. "But the little dudes here haven't seen him for DAYS. It's bad news, man. Poor Glitterpuff. I can't believe he'd do this to such a bodacious señorita. I guess he just didn't wanna get married. Not cool, though, Sal. Not cool."

I felt TERRIBLE that I had thought Glitterpuff was the thief and guinea pig-napper when she wasn't. So I rushed over to the bride.

"Glitterpuff," I said. "I'm so sorry we tried to interview you today."

"Don't worry, Pugly," said Glitterpuff, sniffing. "I couldn't let you in my kennel because I didn't want you to see my wedding dress." And then she started howling again.

"Glitterpuff," I said,
"I am a

BRILLIANT DETECTIVE!

I'll find Big Sal!"

Then I heard a voice. "Ho! Hey! Down here, PUGGLES!" It was the angry guinea pig who'd RUINED a perfectly good top hat by stamping all over it. I wasn't sure I liked him very much. Puggles!

"I've got a job for you," he said. "Me and Sal's mum spent a FORTUNE on this wedding. So if you find him you can tell him that he owes me BIG TIME!"

Glitterpuff sniffed and wiped her long nose with her wedding veil. "And you can tell him from ME that I don't want to see that gorgeous, long, orange hair of his EVER again. He has BROKEN my poor poodle heart!"

And THAT'S when I got another

AMAZING DETECTIVE
BRAIN PING!

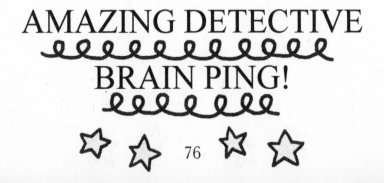

Clem was watching my little pug tail whirling round and round. She knew I thought that I might have just CRACKED THIS CASE.

"What is it, Pugly?" she said.

"Sal's gorgeous, long ORANGE hair. ORANGE. Clem, that's it! ORANGE!"

Clem looked at me, blankly. She had NO IDEA what I was talking about.

So that's when I said, "Almost EVERYTHING that's been stolen is ORANGE. Maddy's fuzzy jumper with the ORANGE pumpkins, Tiny's orange scarf and … wait a minute! Chester! What colour was your new modelling outfit that got stolen?"

"Oh man, I miss that outfit. It was really beautiful, man. Deep orange, like the Californian sunset."

Clem's eyes went wide.

I turned to Glitterpuff and took one of her paws in mine.

"Big Sal DIDN'T run away. He DOES want to marry you. WE WERE RIGHT ALL ALONG. Someone GUINEA PIG-NAPPED him because he's ORANGE! And I know exactly who it was!"

Chapter 11

EVERYONE went MAD when they heard me say Big Sal had been guinea pig-napped!

His family and friends all began squeaking and running round in circles.

"WHO IS IT?" shouted Glitterpuff, rolling up the sleeves of her dress. "I'm going to GET THEM!"

I gulped a bit when I saw Glitterpuff's muscles. She looked like a pink-haired wrestler!

I leaned over and whispered in Clem's ear, "I TOLD you poodles were SCARY!"

Clem stared at Glitterpuff and nodded. "But who IS the thief, Pugly?" she asked.

I couldn't believe that Clem hadn't figured it out yet. A good detective

NOTICES EVERYTHING

and I had just remembered something that I NOTICED during our very first interview.

I looked RIGHT into Clem's eyes and said, "THINK, Clem. WHO spent AGES looking through my pens until she eventually found an ORANGE one. And now it's MISSING from my pencil case!"

Clem's eyes went WIDE and the hair on her back stood up.

"TINY THE CHIHUAHUA!" she cried. And I nodded.

Glitterpuff
went MAD when
she heard my theory.

"Right everyone, LET'S GET MY
FIANCÉ BACK RIGHT NOW!"

And then she stormed down the church
path with hundreds of angry guinea pigs,
some in hats, running after her.

"COME ON, PUGLY,"

said Clem. "We need to get there first!"

"JUMP ON!"

said Chester. That's
when we saw he had a
SKATEBOARD.

"I used to be the San Francisco Dog Skateboarding Champion when I lived in the USA. That was before I started modelling, of course. I couldn't risk an injury after that. Gotta keep this face picture-perfect, you dig me? I mean—"

"CHESTER!" Clem screamed. "Stop YAPPING and start SKATEBOARDING!"

"TOTALLY!"

yelled Chester, excitedly.

"Let's GO!"

And we went RACING down the street past Glitterpuff and the guinea pigs and on to Tiny's house.

Chapter 12

When we arrived at Tiny's house the curtains were still shut tight and she wouldn't answer the door when we rang the doorbell.

"Pugly, we're going round the back," said Clem. "Chester, you stay here and keep watch for Glitterpuff and the guinea pigs. Don't let them come near the house until we find Big Sal."

Then she dashed away round the side of the house.

"You know what, Pugly? I think Clem LIKES me," Chester beamed. "Wanna be

best man at OUR wedding one day?"

I didn't want to say anything to that so I just ran away.

When I got to the back of the house, Clem was already halfway through a small gap in the window. As soon as she was inside she unlocked the door and let me in, too.

Tiny was nowhere to be found.

"Pugly!" hissed Clem. "Stop breathing so loudly! I can hear something."

So I held my breath and listened and that's when I heard whimpering.

"It's coming from downstairs," said Clem. "There must be a basement."

We tried all the doors to see if any of them led down to the basement but they didn't. That's when I spotted a bit of a bump under the rug in the hallway.

"Look," I said. "Trap door!"

And I was right. We pulled the rug back and there it was. A door in the floor.

"Ladies first," I said, gulping.

Clem rolled her eyes at me. "Come on," she said. "Don't be such a scaredy-pug."

So I followed Clem down the little wooden steps into the dark basement.

I couldn't see anything, but I could FEEL a cobweb on my face and that's when

I SCREAMED!

"Who's there?!" said a voice.

Clem and I froze.

It didn't sound like Tiny.

"It's Pugly and Clem," I whispered. "Is that you, Big Sal?"

"Yes, it's me," said the voice.

Big Sal sounded miserable.

"We've come to rescue you," I said. "Where's the light?"

"NO!" cried the voice. "DON'T PUT THE LIGHT ON!"

But Clem had already hit the switch.

Just then Glitterpuff came pounding down the basement stairs.

"I'm sorry, dudes!" yelled Chester from upstairs. "She's REALLY strong. I couldn't stop her."

"SAL!" cried Glitterpuff. "Is that YOU?!"

"DON'T
LOOK
AT ME!"
screamed
Big Sal.

91

But none of us could STOP looking at him because he was almost completely BALD!

"My poor Sal-Sal," said Glitterpuff. "What has that chihuahua DONE to you?!"

Just then a head poked through the trap door. It was Tiny.

"YOU CAN ALL STAY
DOWN THERE
UNTIL THE POLICE GET
HERE AND ARREST YOU
FOR BREAKING
INTO MY HOUSE!"

she yelled, trying to slam the door shut.

So that's when I shouted, "Er, TINY! I think you're forgetting something!"

Tiny opened the trap door and poked her head down.

"What?" she asked.

"When the police get here they'll have to arrest you for being the thief!"

That's when Tiny started crying. And even Clem could see that this time it was real.

"I'm SO SORRY! PLEASE don't send me to doggy jail," whimpered Tiny. "I was just trying to help Big Sal. I thought if I could find the right shade of orange I could colour him in or glue bits of orange stuff to him in time for his wedding day. But nothing worked! And then I suppose I got a bit carried away."

"But why did you GUINEA PIG-NAP him in the first place?" shouted Glitterpuff. "And WHY DID YOU BALD HIM??"

And that's when Tiny looked completely

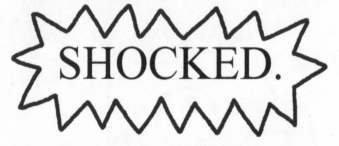

SHOCKED.

"WHAT?! I didn't GUINEA PIG-NAP Sal! And it's DEFINITELY not MY fault he's BALD! He came to ME needing help.

And now he won't LEAVE."

EVERYONE

stared at Big Sal.

"She's telling the truth," he said.

"But we saw the

CRIME SCENE,"

~~~~~~~~~~~~~~~~~~~~~

said Clem. "Your hutch door was wide open and the place was a

MESS."

_____

"I just left in a rush, that's all," said Big Sal.

"But we found

EVIDENCE

_____

that someone else had been in your hutch."

I showed Sal the long, grey hair.

"Get that AWAY FROM ME!" he yelled. "THAT'S the reason I came here!"

Tiny cleared her throat and said, "I've been Big Sal's hairdresser for a while now. You didn't think his hair was THAT thick and shiny without some professional help, did you?"

"WHOA WHOA WHOA! You've never offered to do MY hair before!" said Chester, swishing his hair around. But then he glanced at Sal's patchy, bald bits. "Actually, never mind!" he said.

"So what happened?" Clem asked Tiny. "Did you use the wrong shampoo or something?"

"HEY! It wasn't MY fault," said Tiny. "I tried to get rid of them but nothing worked. I nipped out to get even MORE orange hair dye and when I came back Sal had CUT OFF ALL OF HIS OWN HAIR!"

I was puzzled. "But why?"

"MY HAIR IS TURNING GREY!" wailed Big Sal. "I found the first one in my hutch yesterday," he said, pointing a shaky foot at

EVIDENCE

BAG

ONE.

"I pulled it out and ran over here as FAST as I could. I was worried there were MORE. And there were," he whimpered.

"He's been hiding in my basement ever since he cut all his hair off," said Tiny. "He won't LEAVE!"

That's when Sal turned to Glitterpuff and said, "I know you probably don't want to marry me any more. I mean, I'm NOTHING without my hair."

"Don't be SILLY!" cried Glitterpuff. "It's just HAIR!" And then she picked up the scissors and cut a huge chunk of her own pink hair off and threw it on the ground.

"See? Hair isn't important. I love YOU, Sal, not your hair."

"THEN LET'S GET MARRIED RIGHT NOW!"

screamed Big Sal.

And EVERYONE cheered and ran out of the house.

So that's when me and Clem made Tiny PROMISE that she would take back EVERYTHING that she had stolen and that she'd NEVER steal anything ever again.

"I p-p-promise!" said Tiny.

"Next time we'll call the COPS," said Clem. "Consider yourself WARNED."

"You've caused us a LOT of bother today, Tiny," I said. "I had to give up ALL of my doggy biscuits to keep this investigation going AND I lost my hat in the park!"

"I'm so sorry!" said Tiny. "Here, you can have ALL of my fancy biscuits. I don't deserve them anyway."

So I took a paw-full and then gave the rest of the box back because it had been brave of Tiny to admit what she had done and to apologise.

☆

After the wedding, everyone headed off to
Glitterpuff's kennel for the disco. None of
the other guinea pigs CARED about Big
Sal's hair. In fact, they said it made him
look AS HARD AS NAILS and he

LOVED

that!

By the time me and Clem got home we were so EXHAUSTED that we almost didn't notice the box next to the cat flap.

There was a note on top which said:

"It's probably Maddy's jumper," said Clem.

And it was. But there was something else under the jumper, wrapped up nicely in orange wrapping paper.

I opened it.

It was my DETECTIVE'S HAT!

I looked at Clem. She was just as shocked as I was.

"She must've gone searching for it in the park after I told her I'd lost it! WOW – she must REALLY be sorry."

"Hmm," said Clem. "Maybe chihuahuas aren't that bad after all."

I put my hat back on and went inside with Clem. It was time to write our OFFICIAL REPORT because the case of the missing orange guinea pig had been SOLVED.

And now it was time for belly rubs and BISCUITS!

Bonus Chapter!

Hola Pugly!

Thanks for solving the crime and saving our wedding day! We're having a great time in Mexico. It's really hot so we've both got hats to keep off the sun.

We know how much you love hats so we got you one too!

Love & hugs
Glitterpuff & Sal